If you can...

We can...

Beth Shoshan & Petra Brown

I love you…

… I really do!

(Although my arms are just too small
and so I can't quite cuddle you)

I hug you…
… you hug me

(And round
and round
we dance together,
holding tight.

Don't let me fall!)

I tickle you…

… you giggle too

(But not my toes…! No!
Not my toes,
you know that's when I'll squeal the most!)

I make you laugh …

… you laugh with me

(There's nothing in this world
can make us feel so good
as laughter can, as laughter does,
as laughter should)

I hold your hand…
… you hold mine tight

(Just feeling snug, secure and safe.
Just knowing you'll protect me,
care for me…
… be there)

I sing you songs...
... you sing them too

(Loud ones, soft ones,
make me laugh ones.
Love songs, sleep songs,
safe and sound songs)

I tell you tales…
… you listen close

(Then tell me stories
through the night...

Of mighty dragons,
gallant knights...

adventures made
to fill my mind)

I'm in your dreams…
… and you're
in mine.

(The best dreams, safe dreams,
sleep all night dreams.
My dreams, your dreams.
Always our dreams)

Let's be friends forever, I say!

There for one another,
looking out and taking care.

So...

Whatever you do…

and whatever I do…

Let's do it...

...together!

For you, me and all of us!

B.S.

For Lewis & Samantha

P.B.

First published in 2008
by Meadowside Children's Books
185 Fleet Street
London EC4A 2HS

This edition published 2010 by Little Bee,
an imprint of Meadowside Children's Books

A CIP catalogue record for this book
is available from the British Library

Printed in China

10 9 8 7 6 5 4 3 2